Who's a Bright Girl?

Rose Impey

Who's a bright girl?

Illustrated by

ANDRÉ AMSTUTZ

BARRON'S

New York • Toronto

For Rachel and Charlotte—
two bright girls

First edition for the United States and Canada published 1989
by Barron's Educational Series, Inc.

First published 1985, reprinted 1988 by
William Heinemann, Ltd, Michelin House,
81 Fulham Road, London SW3 6RB

Text © Rose Impey 1985
Illustrations © André Amstutz 1985

All inquiries should be addressed to:
Barron's Educational Series, Inc.
250 Wireless Boulevard
Hauppauge, NY 11788

International Standard Book No. 0-8120-6144-6

Library of Congress Catalog Card No. 89-430

Library of Congress Cataloging-in-Publication Data

Impey, Rose.
    Who's a bright girl?/Rose Impey: illustrated by André
Amstutz.—1st ed. for the U.S. and Canada.
        p.   cm.—(Banana book)
    Summary: A little girl becomes leader of a gang of pirates
after they try to make her their maid, cook, and seamstress.
    ISBN 0-8120-6144-6
    [1. Pirates—Fiction.] I. Amstutz, André, ill. II. Title.
III. Series: Banana book series.
PZ7.I344Wh   1989
[E]—dc19   89-430
                                   CIP
                                   AC

PRINTED IN HONG KONG
901   9903   987654321

The Pirate Gang

IF YOU THINK this is the kind of story where five children, armed with only a bucket and shovel, catch a dangerous band of smugglers, you'd be wrong. And if you think this is the kind of story where a poor, helpless little girl is captured by a terrible gang of cut-throat pirates . . . you'd still be wrong, but a lot closer. Now, those are all the hints I'm going to give you. To find out what happens, you'd better read on . . .

Once upon a time, and not so very long ago, a little girl was walking to school. She was a sensible kind of girl,

who could pack her own lunch and do her mom's shopping without losing the change. She was also far too sensible to talk to strange men whom she met in the street, especially ones with peg legs, scars on their faces, patches over their eyes and scruffy parrots on their shoulders. So when she saw four strange characters fitting this description, she quickly turned the other way and kept on walking.

But the pirates had seen *her*. She was just what they were looking for.

"You look like a sensible little girl," growled the biggest pirate, who was called Jake. "We want a sensible little girl like you to join our gang, don't we, lads?"

"Yes, yes," agreed the rest of the gang, covering their mouths to hide their smiles.

"We're rough, tough pirates and we sail the seas in a mighty, fine pirate ship. We have unusual adventures, don't we, lads?" boasted Jake.

"Oh, yeah, yeah," said the rest of the

gang. They didn't seem quite so sure about this.

"All we need is for you to join us, then we can go off on raids. Isn't that right, lads?" said Jake.

"Yes! Yes!" they agreed, more strongly this time, again covering their mouths to hide their smiles.

Now the little girl knew better than to listen to this kind of story from such wicked-looking villains. She knew they were up to no good. But the idea of having an adventure was far too tempting to miss. She didn't exactly stop, but she walked on more slowly.

"Come on, what do you say? Good Gravy! It would be more fun than going to school, I'm sure," said Jake.

Well, the little girl couldn't argue with that, could she?

She stopped and stared into Jake's big, black eyes.

"Would you really make me into a real pirate?"

"On my honor," swore Jake, trying hard to look honest.

"On my honor"

"Would you give me a real pirate outfit?"

"To be sure, my hearty," said Jake. The other pirates stepped forward and gave her a scarf and a hat and a belt and a patch.

"What about a parrot?" she asked.

For a minute Jake was annoyed, but he settled the parrot on the little girl's shoulder.

"Grilled Gammon! You strike a hard bargain," he snarled. "Now, let's be off. Back to the ship."

The little girl was pleased with herself. The pirates looked happy too. They thought they had tricked her "good and proper." And, if you don't tell the little girl, I'll tell you why.

You see, these pirates were not too happy. They used to sail the seas in a battered ship called *The Leaky Tub*. And it did leak too. The pirates didn't mind, as long as it stayed afloat. Most of the time it did. Then one day they had a piece of luck. They attacked a handsome sailing ship. The crew just ran away and, what's more, they never came back. Jake and his men found themselves the proud owners of *The Flying Dragon*. That was when their problems started.

This ship turned out to be a lot of work. It was sharp-looking and shiny and it seemed a shame not to keep it clean. So Jethro began to wash and scrub the decks. He polished the brass until he could see his face in it. The other pirates liked to see the ship sparkling. It made them feel proud.

There was a cook's galley, with pots and pans and kitchen tools. Joshua liked to cook. He made marvelous meals like seafood risotto, octopus in red wine

and chili sauce, shrimp pancakes and
"The Flying Dragon," a wonderful ice
cream dish with peaches and grapes and
chocolate sauce.

There was also a cabin full of canvas
and sailcloth and needles and thread.
Jem was good at sewing. He could
patch the sails and tack and sew a
seam. He made curtains and cushions
and soon the pirates had new outfits.
They enjoyed looking neat and trim.

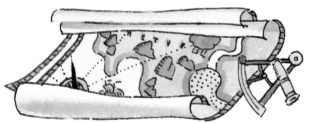

Finally, there was a cozy captain's cabin, with maps and charts. Jake loved to sit in the captain's chair, with his foot up, planning and plotting routes and dreaming about finding buried treasure.

For a while the pirates were happy but soon Jake wanted some adventure. However, the others were always too busy, cleaning and cooking and sewing.

"Jumping Jelly!" Jake roared. "You're turning into a bunch of old women. This isn't a rest home for worn out sailors. We're rough, tough pirates. We should be raiding and rampaging."

The pirates looked ashamed of themselves. But then they said,

"Who's going to cook the meals?"

"Who's going to keep the decks clean?"

"Who will do the sewing and mending?"

"Giant Jam Tarts! That's girl's work," snarled Jake. "We'll get some dumb girl to do these jobs; then we can have adventures."

And that is just what they did, as easy as that. Or so they thought, for they were old-fashioned pirates. They didn't realize that most little girls are too bright to be caught that way. But don't worry, they're going to find out!

The Pirates Find Out

So off they all went, down the road, through the alley, along the path and onto the canal bank. This path ran along the back of the school playing field. The pirates kept their heads down, but the little girl didn't. She would have loved her friends to see her, all dressed up. The pirates couldn't believe how smoothly it had all gone. They thought to themselves, "Are little girls really as dumb as all that?"

When they reached the ship, Jake led the way up the gangplank.

"Welcome aboard *The Flying Dragon*," he said. The little girl was amazed by what she saw. Each of the pirates was impatient to show her what work she would have to do. The little girl was surprised to be so popular.

"Those pirates are up to something," she thought.

First, Jethro showed her the decks and cabins. He showed her the mops and buckets and the polish. He told her all she had to do.

"You'd better do a good job of it. I like to see my face in this brass."

The little girl was surprised. "I'm not doing the cleaning," she thought. "Whoever heard of pirates dusting and polishing?"

Next, Joshua took her to see the cook's galley and showed her the pots and pans.

"We expect good food," he warned her. "No lumps in the potatoes, no

soggy cabbage, no canned soup."

The little girl was even more
surprised. "I'm not doing the cooking,"
she thought. "Whoever heard of pirates
baking?"

Then Jem showed her the tailor's
cabin. He showed her the needles and
thread and rolls of material.

"We like to look good. We can't
have holes in our clothes when we go
off on raids," he said.

The little girl began to look angry.
"I'm not doing the mending," she
thought. "Whoever heard of pirates
sewing?"

She was looking for adventure, and
she was determined to find it.

At last Jake showed her the captain's

cabin. He showed her all his maps and charts. The little girl's eyes widened. Her fingers began to itch.

"Curdled custard! Keep your female fingers off those charts!" he shouted. "You can come in here to flick a dustrag around, if you're careful, but don't touch anything. Plotting and planning is my job and you'd better keep out of my way."

Now the little girl was really angry. She stared into Jake's big, black eyes.

"Did you really think I was going to join a pirate gang to do the cooking and cleaning? You must think I am stupid. Girls don't have to do that kind of thing. Girls can have adventures just like boys. In fact, girls can have better adventures because they are even brighter than boys." And just to prove it she thought of a clever plan.

The pirates were surprised and disappointed. If girls didn't do this kind of thing, who was going to cook and clean and sew? It seemed they still had their problem after all. The little girl looked at their puzzled faces.

"Don't worry, I know how we can figure this out. We can all have a vote. That way we all decide who should do each job," she said.

The pirates were completely confused. They had never come across this idea before. She tried to explain. "We vote for the best person for each job. Then at the end, everyone is happy.

"First," said the little girl, in her teacher's voice, "who makes delicious doughnuts, tasty pies and perfect puddings? Who should do the cooking?"

The pirates began to feel hungry.

They all turned to Joshua and pointed at him.

"Good," said the little girl. "Then that's decided and *everyone* is happy." Joshua didn't look happy; he looked puzzled, but all the others were smiling. They didn't have to do the cooking.

"Now," said the little girl, "who can make the brass brightest and the decks shiniest? Who should do the cleaning?"

The pirates liked their sparkling ship.

They all turned to Jethro and pointed to him.

"Good," said the little girl, "then that's decided and *everyone* is happy."

Jethro didn't look happy; he looked puzzled, but all the others were smiling. They didn't have to do the cleaning.

"Next," said the little girl, "who can sew a straight seam and patch a pair of pants? Who should do the sewing?" The pirates were proud of their fine clothes. They all turned to Jem and pointed at him.

"Good," said the little girl, "then that's decided and *everyone* is happy."

Jem didn't look happy, he looked puzzled, but all the others were smiling. They didn't have to do the sewing.

"Finally," said the little girl, "we must

choose the captain. This is an important job."

Jake was smiling. He liked being the captain and giving orders. He enjoyed having plenty of time to plot and plan and dream about buried treasure.

But the little girl went on, "Who is the bossiest person on this ship? Who is the best at telling other people what to do? Who is bright and smart and good at getting their own way? Who should be the captain?"

All the others turned to Jake. He was certainly bossy. Then they looked at the little girl. She was far more bossy and smarter than Jake. They all pointed at her.

"Good," said the little girl, "then

that's decided and *everyone* is happy.
You can be the captain's mate," she said
to Jake.

Jake wasn't happy; he was hopping
mad, but what could he do?

"Now back to work you lazy good-
for-nothings," she shouted, "and be
quick about it."

The pirates disappeared and soon the ship began to move. *The Flying Dragon* glided along the canal bank until it came to a fork where it joined the wide river. Gathering speed, it sailed down the river until, as the sun was setting, it reached the open sea.

The little girl sat in the captain's chair with her feet on the captain's table. She couldn't believe how smoothly it has gone.

Are pirates really as stupid as that? she wondered.

Adventures at Sea

SOON THE LITTLE girl and Jake were
busy planning raids. They made attacks
on other ships, when they could tempt
the pirates away from their cooking and
cleaning. They climbed the rigging. They
manned the cannons. They hoisted the
sails and went in search of adventure.

Their first victory was over a tough
seadog called Captain Crackers. Some
people said he was 105 years old. You
would never have guessed it to see him
swing from the rigging with a knife

between his teeth. But after he met the little girl he decided to retire.

Next, they got the better of a well-known villain, Captain Cutthroat.

"I'll slice you up and feed you to the sharks," he said. But things didn't work out like that. He was made to walk the plank, along with the rest of his crew.

Their greatest adventure was when they were attacked by a black-hearted pirate called Captain Bonnet. He and his scurvy crew came aboard *The Flying Dragon* with pistols at the ready, but the ship seemed to be deserted. Jake and his men were hiding. They often did this when the fighting got too fierce. The little girl had climbed the tallest mast. She cut free a huge sail which fell to the deck, trapping the pirates underneath.

Now Jake and the pirates could see what little girls were made of.

After a while the pirates needed a rest. They wanted to get the place ship-shape again. But the little girl had a real taste for adventure now. She was preparing a new plan, to make a pirate raid on her school.

She would terrify the teachers and scare the secretary. She would capture the custodian and chase the children around the playground. She would take the school by storm and force the principal to walk the plank!
She was very excited about this plan.

But the other pirates were not too happy about it.

"Whoever heard of pirates attacking a school full of kids," grumbled Jake, who was getting fed up with the little girl and her bright ideas.

"That's why it's such a good idea,"

said the little girl, "Because nobody would expect it. The element of surprise."

But there would be nothing to steal. "Who wants hundreds of rulers and pairs of rusty scissors?" said Jethro.

"Ah, but on Mondays there's lots of money. It takes the secretary all morning to count it. I've seen her. Piles of it all over her table."

The little girl wasn't really interested in the money; it was glory she wanted, but she had to keep the pirates happy.

"There's only five of us. There must be hundreds of them," said Joshua.

"They don't count," said the little girl, who felt like a real pirate by now. They're just a bunch of kids and a few teachers. They'd be no problem."

None of the pirates looked convinced. They thought it was a crazy idea. The little girl could see she had a problem. She changed her tactics.

"Okay, who is in charge around here? Who was chosen to be the captain of this ship? Who makes the decisions?" she said.

All the pirates turned and pointed at her. They knew when they were beaten.

"Good," said the little girl, "then that's decided and *everyone* is happy."

"Really," she thought, "pirates are very stupid."

"School Ahoy!"

ON MONDAY MORNING, as the sun begin to rise, *The Flying Dragon* left the open sea and sailed into the mouth of the wide river. Soon it reached the fork where the river joined the canal. It glided along the canal until, at last, the school came into view.

"School ahoy!" called the little girl. "Weigh anchor, lads."

School ahoy!

The pirates lowered the gangplank and left the ship. They crept across the playing field and entered the school porch. The little girl pushed the front door open and they all peered inside. It was about 11 o'clock. The children had just returned from morning recess and the school was very quiet. Every sound seemed to echo down the tiled hall.

The little girl felt nervous to be coming into school at this time. It was like having been to the dentist and coming back late, feeling strange and shy. But she found herself carried along by the others. They just wanted to get it over with and get back to the ship. They felt uncomfortable on dry land.

In the front hall a display of dinosaur models was gathering dust. Footprints in chalk dust led all the way into the boys' coatroom.

"What a fine mess," said Jethro. "Doesn't anyone keep this place clean?"

While the others were arguing in which direction to go, he took off his scarf and began to polish the brass handles on the front door.

"Oh, dear, stewed cabbage and burned rice pudding, I would guess," said Joshua. He followed a terrible smell which drifted along the hall from the school kitchen. Peeping through an open classroom door, Jem could see a sewing group waiting patiently while someone's mom threaded needles for a long line of children. He thought he would go in and give her a hand.

By the time the little girl and Jake entered the secretary's office they had

lost the rest of the gang. Miss Crow,
the school secretary, was arranging an
enormous heap of money into neat piles
and scribbling numbers on the edge of her
blotter. She looked tired and
irritable. She kept sighing and
scratching her head.

They waited for her to look up from her counting but she didn't. Finally she spoke, "Put it down on the table," and then, "Thank you!"

When Jake moved forward at the sight of so much money, she snapped, "Keep those fat little fingers off my money." He jumped back in alarm, looking guiltily at his hands.

Off!

The little girl decided to take over, "We've come for the money," she said. Miss Crow was not impressed. She still didn't look up.

"Well, it isn't ready yet," she said. "And don't use that tone with me. Really, I've only one pair of hands, you know. It's always the same on a Monday. Rush, rush, rush. I do the

best I can and if it isn't good enough . . .
well . . . I'm sorry but . . ."

The little girl and Jake backed out of
the secretary's office and closed the
door quietly. They both felt guilty.

"Curdled custard!" whispered Jake,
and the little girl nodded in agreement.

At that moment they heard a voice coming from the hall, which the little girl recognized. It was the voice of Mrs. Raven, the principal. She didn't sound at all happy either.

"No, no, no, that's hopeless," she said in a tired voice. "You're supposed to be fierce and bloodthirsty. You wouldn't frighten a rice pudding. If only we had some real pirates," she said, "Then we might see some action."

At this, the little girl and Jake began to feel better. They drew their pirate pistols and rushed into the hall.

"Abandon ship, you miserable varmints, or we'll string you from the flag pole," roared the little girl. Children flew screaming in all directions. Some of them hid behind Mrs. Raven.

The little girl looked at them. They were children she knew and they were all wearing pirate outfits. She felt cheated. She stared open-mouthed at them while they stared back at her. It wasn't fair. She was speechless.

But Mrs. Raven was delighted. "Oh, well done, Mary Mansfield! That's more like it. We must find a part for you in our play." The children were

crowding around her and Mrs. Raven
was patting her on the back.

"That's what I wanted, children, a
really bold pirate voice. You've got to
sound like pirates, as well as looking
like them. Your . . . er . . . friend looks
the part," she said politely, turning
to Jake. "Perhaps you might be able to
advise us on our costumes, Mr. . . . ?"

"Jake Juggins, at your service, your

honor," said Jake, shaking hands roughly with the principal. Seeing the little girl busy with her friends, he added, "*Captain* of *The Flying Dragon*."

Mrs. Raven sent the children back to their classrooms. Then she explained to Jake that they were practicing for the Christmas play. They were doing *Peter Pan*. Mrs. Raven told Jake she was having problems with the pirates. Jake gave her lots of advice. He told her what the pirates should wear and the kinds of things they should say. A few of these ideas were not quite suitable, but Mrs. Raven was far too tactful to say so.

At lunchtime the little girl went to look for the pirates. She found Joshua in the school kitchen, helping to serve lunch. Jethro was telling the school caretaker how to get a better shine on the hall floor. Jem was teaching two young boys how to sew buttons back on their coats. They'd been having a fight in the playground.

Peeping through the office window, she spotted Jake, who was now having a cup of tea with the principal. Mrs. Raven had a selection of maps and a huge globe. There were countries marked that Jake had never even heard of.

"Great Goulash, your worship," said Jake, who had never met a principal before, "you run a splendid ship, if I may be so bold."

Great Goulash

As for Mary Mansfield, she was happy to be back. She became the heroine of the school. She was glad she hadn't missed the play. She was sure to get the part of Captain Hook. All her friends wanted to hear about her adventures. She told them how she captured a band of cutthroat pirates single-handed, became their captain, led raids on enemy ships and collected enough treasure to sink a school. At last, when she got tired of the life, she had tricked the pirates into bringing her home. And to prove it—here she was.

She discovered that telling the stories was nearly as good as having the adventures. She thought she might be a writer when she grew up. She already had lots of ideas. She was, after all, a very bright little girl. But then, most girls are, in my experience.